Jakers!™

Piggley
Makes a Friend

adapted by Wendy Wax
images by Entara Ltd.

Ready-to-Read

Simon Spotlight
New York London Toronto Sydney

Based on the TV series *Jakers! The Adventures of Piggley Winks* created by Entara Ltd.

SIMON SPOTLIGHT
An imprint of Simon & Schuster Children's Publishing Division
1230 Avenue of the Americas, New York, New York 10020

Manufactured in the United States of America
First Edition
2 4 6 8 10 9 7 5 3 1
Library of Congress Cataloging-in-Publication Data
Wax, Wendy.
Piggley makes a friend / adapted by Wendy Wax ; images by Entara Ltd. — 1st ed.
p. cm. — (Ready-to-read)
"Based on the TV series Jakers!, the adventures of Piggley Winks, created by Entara Ltd. as seen on PBS Kids."
ISBN-13: 978-1-4169-3581-0
ISBN-10: 1-4169-3581-9
I. Entara Ltd. II. Jakers, the adventures of Piggley Winks (Television program) III. Title.
PZ7.W35117Pi 2007
2007003015

It was a spring day.

The  was shining.
SUN

 looked outside.
PIGGLEY

"Today is a fine day,"

said .
MR. HORNSBY

"We will take our lesson

outside in the ."
SUN

"We will look

for , and .

FLOWERS   LEAVES   ANIMALS

We will work

in teams of two."

"Can I work with or ?"

DANNAN   FERNY

asked .

PIGGLEY

"Not today," said .

MR. HORNSBY

"Today we will all work

with someone new.

You will work with  ."

HECTOR

 did not want

PIGGLEY

to work with .

HECTOR

 thought

PIGGLEY HECTOR

was bossy.

"Follow me!" said  .

HECTOR

But 🐷 did not want

PIGGLEY

to follow 🦡 .

HECTOR

🐷 was used to

PIGGLEY

being in charge.

"I see a squirrel!"  said.
PIGGLEY

"Let me take a 🖼️."
PICTURE

"No!" said 🐾.
HECTOR

He grabbed the .
CAMERA

"I see a TOAD.

We should take a PICTURE

of the TOAD."

"Give me the CAMERA !" said PIGGLEY.

"No!" said HECTOR.

"Look! DEER !" shouted PIGGLEY.

"Let me take a PICTURE !" said HECTOR.

"I saw them first!" said .
PIGGLEY

They both grabbed the .
CAMERA

The  made a loud **click**.
CAMERA

The  made a bright flash.
CAMERA

The  ran away.
DEER

"The  were scared away!"

said .

"We need to find them!

I see  tracks.

We can follow the tracks

to find the !"

 went off to find the .
HECTOR   DEER

 stopped to take
PIGGLEY

a  of a 🐟.
PICTURE   FISH

Then he ran after .
                    HECTOR

Soon they came to an old castle.

 tried to take a .

PIGGLEY   PICTURE

 grabbed the .

HECTOR   CAMERA

"Give it back!" said .

PIGGLEY

They heard a loud sound.

"What is that?" asked .

PIGGLEY

"That is the cry of a baby ,"

DEER

said .

HECTOR

"My mother and I

heard a baby cry
DEER

when we went for a walk

in the forest."

"You did?" asked  .
PIGGLEY

PIGGLEY did not know that **HECTOR**

liked to go for walks

with his mother.

There was a lot about **HECTOR**

that **PIGGLEY** did not know.

 took a of

HECTOR PICTURE

with the .

PIGGLEY DEER

Then they walked back

to  together.

SCHOOL

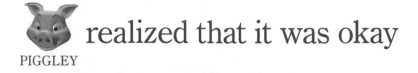 PIGGLEY realized that it was okay

to not always be in charge.

They had to work together

to get the job done.

"We make a good team,"

 told .

PIGGLEY   HECTOR

"Yes, we do!" said .

HECTOR

liked the .

MR. HORNSBY PICTURES

But most of all,

he was happy that

 and were friends.

PIGGLEY HECTOR